PUFFIN BOOKS

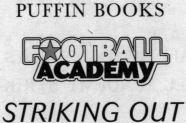

STRIKING OUT

Tom Palmer is a football fan and a writer. He never did well at school. But once he got into reading about football – in newspapers, magazines and books – he decided he wanted to be a football writer more than anything. As well as the Football Academy series, he is the author of the Football Detective series, also for Puffin Books.

Tom lives in a Yorkshire town called Todmorden with his wife and daughter. The best stadium he's visited is Real Madrid's Santiago Bernabéu.

Find out more about Tom on his website *tompalmer.co.uk*

TOM **PALMER**

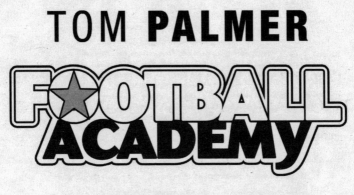

STRIKING OUT

Illustrated by
Brian Williamson

PUFFIN

PUFFIN BOOKS

Published by the Penguin Group
Penguin Books Ltd, 80 Strand, London WC2R ORL, England
Penguin Group (USA) Inc., 375 Hudson Street, New York, New York 10014, USA
Penguin Group (Canada), 90 Eglinton Avenue East, Suite 700, Toronto, Ontario, Canada M4P 2Y3
(a division of Pearson Penguin Canada Inc.)
Penguin Ireland, 25 St Stephen's Green, Dublin 2, Ireland (a division of Penguin Books Ltd)
Penguin Group (Australia), 250 Camberwell Road, Camberwell, Victoria 3124, Australia
(a division of Pearson Australia Group Pty Ltd)
Penguin Books India Pvt Ltd, 11 Community Centre, Panchsheel Park, New Delhi – 110 017, India
Penguin Group (NZ), 67 Apollo Drive, Rosedale, North Shore 0632, New Zealand
(a division of Pearson New Zealand Ltd)
Penguin Books (South Africa) (Pty) Ltd, 24 Sturdee Avenue, Rosebank, Johannesburg 2196, South Africa

Penguin Books Ltd, Registered Offices: 80 Strand, London WC2R ORL, England

puffinbooks.com

First published 2009
017

Text copyright © Tom Palmer, 2009
Illustrations copyright © Brian Williamson, 2009
All rights reserved

The moral right of the author and illustrator has been asserted

Set in 14/21 pt Baskerville MT
Typeset by Palimpsest Book Production Limited, Grangemouth, Stirlingshire
Made and printed in England by Clays Ltd, St Ives plc

British Library Cataloguing in Publication Data
A CIP catalogue record for this book is available from the British Library

ISBN: 978-0-141-32468-5

www.greenpenguin.co.uk

For David Luxton, genius literary agent
and Leeds fan

Contents

Leading Scorer

Yunis trapped the ball with his left foot and looked up. He had a second to decide: play the ball back to Jake, or try to chip the keeper and half of his defence.

He'd been practising chipping at home in the garden. But only when his dad was out. If he got the right backspin on the ball, he could send it over the washing line, on to the roof of his dad's shed and have it bounce back to his feet.

Now was his chance to try it out for real.

Before the first defender reached him, he caught the underside of the ball hard with the top of his boot. It lofted high, then plunged downwards at speed, beating everyone. The net shook as the ball nestled at the back of the goal.

The keeper hadn't bothered moving. There was nothing he could have done. Yunis had scored his best goal yet. His third in this game. A second hat-trick for United.

Jake was the first over to him, jumping on his back. Then Chi and James ran up from defence. Arms clasped his shoulder. Hands rubbed the top of his head. Even Craig came over and slapped his back, which surprised Yunis.

Craig was the one player he'd not really got to know yet. He was quiet and didn't really mix with the others. Except he wasn't quiet on the pitch. On the pitch you couldn't miss him – sometimes he overdid it with his hard tackles.

Everyone was speaking to Yunis at once.

'Brilliant!'

'Awesome.'

'Fantastic goal.'

Yunis came out from under the scrum of his team-mates. He looked at the players'

parents standing in a long row on the touchline. All of them were applauding him. Even the parents of the Wigan players.

This was United under-twelves' fourth game of the season.

The season had started badly with two defeats. There were three new players in the team and it had taken time for them to get used to each other. Yunis was one of those new players, along with Jake and Will. This was their first season playing for a Premiership club academy and it had taken a few games for things to gel.

But in the third game United had gone to City and won four–nil. And now they were coasting it at home to Wigan.

It was five–one. And Yunis's goal total for the season so far was eight.

He couldn't believe this was happening to him.

The first thing he did every time he got to the Academy on a Sunday was check the team sheet, pinned on the wall. And every time he read it, there was his name: Yunis Khan. Wearing the number nine shirt.

But, even with all these good things happening, deep down Yunis wasn't completely happy. Because when he'd looked at the row of parents, all clapping

5

and cheering him, there was one set of parents missing.

His.

It was always the same: Yunis's mum and dad never came to watch him play.

But that wasn't going to stop him.

If anything, the more upset it made him feel, the better he played.

Five minutes later, Yunis saw Jake pick the ball up wide on the halfway line. He knew what would happen next. They'd talked about this – and practised it. So he jogged towards the other wing, keeping level with the last defender, thirty yards out.

Jake tapped the ball to Chi, who turned and fed the ball down the touchline. Jake was on to it like a flash. The perfect one-two. Three touches, at pace, and Jake was level with the eighteen-yard box.

Then suddenly Yunis sprinted towards the far post, losing his marker easily.

Jake looked up and crossed the ball, curling it on to Yunis's head.

Yunis directed it down to his right.

Goal.

Six–one.

The Wigan keeper on the ground again.

And all the United parents cheering and clapping.

The Getaway

Yunis saw the referee check his watch and pull his whistle out. He was waiting for that. Waiting for the chance to get off the pitch. Quickly.

Three long blasts on the whistle were followed by more loud applause from the parents. Two big wins on the trot was good. Things were going well for the Academy's under-twelves. *And* for Yunis.

Yunis looked at the parents, each walking towards their son. Jake's dad calling

Yunis over. Yunis waved back at him, but kept on going.

It was nice of Jake's dad to try to congratulate him, but Yunis wanted to get to the dressing rooms as soon as he could. It would have been satisfying to take all the praise he knew he'd get if he hung around. But the fact that his dad wasn't there – and everybody else's was – made him feel sad.

He just wanted to get away.

As he walked off, only one father and son were ahead of him: James and his dad.

James's dad was the former United player and England international Cyril Cunningham.

James was the only player at United's Academy whose dad had been an international footballer. There were a couple who had lower-league dads. And a few with top-flight grandads. But James's dad was the most impressive. He had seventeen caps for his country. He'd even played in the World Cup. And he was famous for being the second-ever black player to play for England.

Yunis saw that James's dad had his arm round his son. He was coaching him. Yunis could tell. And he could imagine what he was saying. Running him through all the good things he'd done. Highlighting the

things he could work on to become a better player.

He slowed down, so he didn't catch up with them.

He had to admit it to himself: he was jealous. Sick-as-a-dog jealous.

Yunis had nearly made it to the dressing rooms, when he heard a voice behind him. Craig's voice.

Yunis kept walking. It was strange for

Craig to be talking to him. He'd expected
to hear Jake's voice. Or Will's. For one
thing he knew Craig would be with his dad.
He was always with his dad. Theirs was
another of the father–son relationships he
envied.

'Yunis? Yunis?' Craig was calling again.

He had to look round. *If someone calls
your name, you must answer them.* That's what
his dad always said. *It would be disrespectful
not to.*

So Yunis stopped, turned round and
smiled. Craig *was* with his dad. It was
uncanny how similar they looked. Both tall
and broad-shouldered. Both with a mess
of wiry hair. Yunis had heard Jake talk
about Craig's family. They were all like
that.

'Well done, son,' the man said. 'You
played a stormer today. That third goal.

When you chipped the keeper. Brilliant.
How did you pull that off?'

Yunis smiled, then shrugged.

'Your dad not here? Your mum?'
Craig's dad said, looking back at the crowd
of parents and players moving towards
them across the fields. 'I bet they'll wish
they'd not missed this one.'

'No,' Yunis said. 'They . . .'

'They're never here,' Craig said, 'are
they, Yunis?'

As soon as Craig spoke, Yunis felt a pressure in his head. A hot feeling. He was convinced that Craig was having a go at him, taking the mick. And he wasn't having that.

So he just turned his back and walked away.

His dad would have been furious with him. *Never turn your back on someone while they're talking to you.*

But Yunis was sick of his dad's rules.

He was feeling bad enough anyway.

And the worst thing was, he could hear Craig and his dad talking.

'What's the matter with him?'

'He's a . . . ' Yunis didn't catch what Craig had said.

Yunis walked more quickly. Angry. Confused. Lonely. And feeling like he hated everybody and everything.

Sunday 16 October
United 6 Wigan 1
Goals: Yunis (4), Jake, Will
Bookings: Craig

Under-twelves manager's marks out of ten
for each player:

Tomasz	6
Connor	6
James	7
Ryan	7
Craig	5
Chi	6
Sam	7
Will	7
Jake	8
Yunis	10
Ben	7

On Form

'**A**re you all right?'

It was Jake. He sat down next to Yunis in the dressing rooms. Yunis was almost changed.

Yunis knew Jake better than anyone. They'd met at the trials for the under-twelves earlier in the autumn. And they'd hit it off. On the pitch and off it.

'I'm fine,' Yunis said, grinning at his friend.

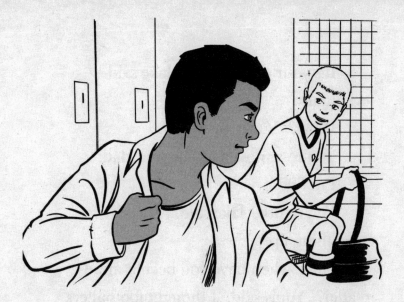

'You were great today. That chip. It was awesome.'

'You set the other three up,' Yunis said. 'So it's thanks to you.'

'Thanks,' Jake said. 'You should have hung around though – everyone was raving about you after the game. The Wigan manager especially. I think he wants to poach you.'

Yunis smiled, but said nothing. And neither did Jake for a minute.

'It's your dad, isn't it?' Jake said eventually.

'What?' Yunis answered.

'You're annoyed about your dad.'

'I'm fine.'

'You're not,' Jake said. 'There's something up.'

'Since when have you been a mind-reader?' Yunis said. 'I thought footballers were supposed to be stupid.'

Jake laughed.

Yunis felt OK talking to Jake about this. 'He's just never here,' Yunis said. 'And he's always going on about how much he hates football . . . And Mum never comes either – because she knows he's so against it.'

'He'll come round,' Jake said.

'But he won't.' Yunis had that feeling again. The pressure in his head. He kept his voice low. 'You don't understand. Your dad's about as good as a dad can get. Mine's rubbish. Imagine if your dad wasn't there to say how well you'd done. Even to criticize you. I'd be happy even if he was here saying how rubbish I was. I'd be happier than this.'

But Jake had stopped listening. He was staring at the other side of the dressing room. There was an argument between some of the other players.

Yunis looked to where the commotion was coming from.

Ryan was at it again. Having a go at Tomasz.

Ryan was the team captain. And a bit of a bully at times. Jake had had a run-in with him earlier in the season, but they'd sorted their differences out. But Ryan was forever having a go at Tomasz, United's keeper, who came from Poland.

'Say "goalkeeper",' Ryan said.

'Golkeeper,' Tomasz said, playing along.

'It's "goal", not "gol",' Ryan laughed.

'Gol.'

Ryan sneered. 'Say "that".'

'Zat.'

Ryan was getting louder and louder. And Tomasz was getting more and more frustrated. Yunis worried about what could

happen next. He wondered if Tomasz
would ever hit Ryan. Probably not.

But Yunis was so cross about it – on top
of everything else – that he felt like hitting
Ryan himself. He was just about to stand up
and tell Ryan to stop, when Steve Cooper
– the under-twelves manager – came into
the dressing room.

Ryan stopped winding Tomasz up
immediately.

Steve Cooper was a man of medium

height with dark straggly hair and a deep booming voice. Most of the lads really liked him. But no one messed him about.

'Right, lads,' Steve said. 'That was brilliant. Thank you. I really enjoyed that performance.'

The boys were sitting in a four-sided dressing room, benches round three of the sides and a row of showers in a long cubicle. They were all trying to look serious, as if they were listening to his words and taking them in. But most of them couldn't help grinning. It was good to be praised. Especially by Steve. He'd even thanked them!

'Yunis. Four goals. That was excellent. In fact, all of you forwards and midfielders did well. Those moves we practised last week. The passing. Does it make sense?'

Half the team muttered yes. All of them nodded.

'But the defence. That was the heart of it. Well led, Ryan. Really good. And Tomasz. Those early saves set up the win. Well done, all of you.'

Steve glanced at his clipboard.

'Oh yes, I wanted to remind those of you who haven't come back with the signed slip from your parents, that the deadline for confirming a place on the Poland trip, during the school holidays, is a week on Monday.'

Yunis glanced at Tomasz who was grinning. He knew Tomasz would be happy about going back to Poland.

James and Chi began rummaging in their bags, looking for the signed forms that permitted them to go with the club to take part in a tournament against several European under-twelves teams. *Including* Real Madrid.

'If I don't get the slips,' Steve said, 'then you can't come. It's as simple as that. If anyone needs to talk about it, you know where I am. OK, another thing . . .'

Yunis had switched off from the rest of what Steve had to say.

He'd not even shown the letter about Poland to his mum and dad. There was no way they would let him go – even though it was during the school holidays. Nor had he told Steve he had a problem with it. He'd just ignored it. So now he definitely had a problem.

Should he show his dad the letter tonight?

What was the point? He had no chance.

Home Truths

'**W**ould you pass the salt, Yunis, please?'

Yunis picked up a cut-glass salt-cellar and handed it to his father.

'Thank you.'

Yunis's dad had picked him up outside the United training ground after Monday-night training as usual, then brought him home. Now they were having their evening family meal in the dining room, the table set, napkins on their knees, the television off.

Just how his dad liked it.

The room was small, with just enough space for the dining table and four chairs. There was a huge sideboard along the far side of the room, displaying plates and family photographs.

Yunis knew most of his mates had their dinner in front of the TV. But his dad always insisted on this. Every night.

'Did you have a good day at school, Jasminder?' Mum said to Yunis's sister.

'Yes, thank you. We wrote a story in English. And Miss Page said mine was very good.'

Yunis sat quietly. Today he was angry with *both* his parents. And his sister, come to that. This meal where they had to talk to each other was so annoying. They were playing at being a happy family, but all he could think about was how his mum and dad never came to watch him at United. How happy did that make *him* feel?

'Well done, love,' Mum said. 'And what about you, Yunis? What did you do today?'

'School,' Yunis said. 'Then training.' He wondered about showing his mum the letter about Poland now, but decided against it.

'And what did you *do* at school, Yunis?' Dad said.

'Maths. Chemistry. And French.'

Yunis knew it was just a matter of time

before his short answers would wind his dad
up. Then they'd have an argument. That
was how it had been recently. So today he
decided to start the argument himself.

'Dad?'

'Yes, son.'

'Please will you come to watch me at
the Academy?'

Yunis's dad put down his knife and fork
and wiped his mouth with his napkin. He
looked at Yunis, pausing.

'We've talked about this.'

'But I want you to come. Just once. Everyone else's dads are there. They –'

'Did you do well today, Yunis?' Mum asked.

Yunis knew what his mum was doing: trying to *stop* the argument.

'Steve, the manager, says he's really pleased with the team. We won six–one yesterday. I scored four goals.'

'That's all very well,' Dad said. He was angry now, ignoring Yunis's point that he had done better than ever in a United shirt. 'But how did you do in maths, chemistry and French? *Not* so well. Your last marks were not as good as they were when you weren't at your football place. I've been talking to your school.'

Yunis frowned. He looked at his sister – who seemed to be enjoying the argument – and scowled at her.

'I am very unhappy about it,' Dad continued. 'When do you do your homework? You leave school at three thirty? Yes?'

'Three,' Yunis said.

'But you don't finish football until eight?'

'Yes.'

'So much time lost. What do you do with it? And two evenings a week. And Sundays. I said this would happen.'

'I do work when I get there,' Yunis said. 'When I can.'

'Yes, in a corridor. On a bench outside. Men in boots clattering and shouting around you. You need a table. You need quiet.'

'I try to make up the time. On the other days.'

'Yes, you try. But you are always

behind, Yunis. Your teacher told me. You are behind.'

Yunis looked at his mum. He wanted her to step in. Defend him. But she continued to look down at her plate.

'I am worried, Yunis. I have to admit it. I am watching. If your results in school work don't change – if Mr Day at the school does not tell me there is improvement – I will have to think about withdrawing you from United.'

Yunis felt the blood rush to his head. 'But you said I could have a year.' He realized that he was shouting. 'To try it.'

He looked at his mum again.

'Only if your schooling didn't suffer,' Dad said. 'And it *is* suffering.'

Yunis stared at *his* plate now. He had so many things he wanted to say to his dad. But he knew there was no point. His dad hated football, hated the fact that he was playing at the Academy. He was just looking for an excuse to make Yunis give it up.

He touched the letter from Steve in his pocket. He realized that he was stupid to think either his mum or his dad would ever be in the right mood to look at it.

All his thoughts were swirling around. Images of his team-mates with their dads' arms around them filled his head. He was confused. He wanted to shout even louder at his dad.

And then he said it.

It just came out.

'If you were bothered about me you'd let me carry on at United. Because you'd know that it's all I've ever wanted. But you aren't, are you?'

Football v School

Dad was quiet for too long.

It was better when he started shouting straight away.

Mum and Jasminder looked at each other. But not at Yunis.

No one looked at Yunis. Not even Dad, when he finally started talking.

'Do you know what the most important thing in the world is?' Dad said in a quiet voice – so quiet it was frightening.

Yunis said nothing. He knew that these

weren't questions he was meant to answer.

'Education,' said his dad, looking at his
wife.

Mum nodded, finally looking at Yunis.

'How do you think we can afford
this house?' his dad said. 'The car that I
ferry you around in? The holidays? Your
clothes? Your things?' His voice was still
quiet.

Again, there was no need for an answer.
Anyway, Yunis knew the answer.

'Education,' Dad said. 'My education. Your grandfather and grandmother had almost nothing. But what they did have was the knowledge that they should give me and your uncles a good education.'

'I know,' Yunis said. 'And I like school. I want an education.'

Yunis's dad pushed his unfinished dinner aside and he leaned towards his son.

'This football is taking up too much of your time. Football is not for me. You know that. But I am genuinely happy that it makes you happy. Because – although *you* have just said that I'm not – I am *bothered* about you. But it is *because* I am bothered about you . . .'

Yunis watched his dad pause, look down at his hands, then take a sip from his water.

'Football is fun,' Dad continued after

a minute. 'But how many players become professional?'

'Not many,' Yunis said, grudgingly.

'And that is what I am worried about. You. Your future. You need your education first. Then, if there is time, the football. Because it is something you love.'

'I can do both,' Yunis said.

'Can you?'

'I can. I will. I promise.'

Dad looked into Yunis's eyes. Yunis

tried to read his mind. What was he going to say? He couldn't work it out. He could quite easily say that it was over: that Yunis would have to leave United.

'We'll give it some more time, Yunis,' Dad said. 'If, by Christmas, you are still not keeping up with your work, then, I'm sorry . . .'

Yunis sighed.

After that, Dad talked to Mum about his job, as Jasminder made faces at Yunis.

As soon as he could, Yunis left the table. He wanted to be in his room.

Dad's Secret

After his parents had gone to bed, Yunis flicked his desk lamp on. The clock said ten past midnight.

He pulled a book out of his school bag and began to read it. Shakespeare. *Macbeth*.

He'd never got on with this sort of thing. Why did he have to read a book written by someone who'd been dead for

four hundred years? How was it supposed
to mean anything to him?

He started reading where he'd left off:

Is this a dagger, which I see before me,
The handle towards my hand? Come let me
    clutch thee:
I have thee not, and yet I see thee still.
Art thou not, fatal vision, sensible . . .

Yunis tried to remember what the teacher had said about it. All the things he was supposed to look out for.

But nothing came into his mind. Just confusion and the feeling that he was reading a foreign language.

The teacher had said to him that he should read it a page at a time, then read the notes about what the words meant, then read it again and try to make sense of it all.

So he began.

Half an hour later – two pages on – Yunis heard a noise.

Someone on the landing.

He turned the light off and didn't move.

His door opened gently and Yunis saw his mum looking in. He tried to stay still, hoping she wouldn't notice him sat rigid at his desk – and not asleep in bed.

'Yunis?' whispered Mum.

Yunis said nothing.

'Yunis. You're scaring me. Is that you?'

He flicked his lamp on. Mum was squinting back at him.

'What are you doing?' she whispered. 'It's nearly one in the morning.'

'Reading this.' Yunis showed her the book.

Mum pulled a face.

'Can't you sleep?' she asked gently.
Then she looked like she'd realized why he
was reading in the middle of the night.

'Oh, Yunis. You mustn't do this. You'll
tire yourself out.'

Five minutes later they were both in the
kitchen, a large room with yellow wallpaper
and wooden fittings surrounding a kitchen
table and four chairs. Two cups of hot
chocolate steamed in front of them.

'You know your dad is doing this
because he thinks it's the right thing?'

'Of course I do, Mum. But . . .'

'But you want to be a footballer?'

'Yes.'

'But your dad told you –'

'I know. I know most boys don't make
it. But at least I have a chance.' Yunis

looked at his mum. 'I just don't understand. He can see I'm trying hard at school too. Maybe I'm just not as clever as he thinks I am. Not as clever as *him*.'

Mum sat back in her chair. She looked sad. Yunis thought she might cry.

'Can I tell you a story?' she said.

'Yes,' Yunis said. 'As long as Macbeth's not in it.'

Mum smiled.

'When your dad was a boy he used to watch United,' she said.

'What? Dad? You're joking me.'

'No. He was a big fan. He had posters on his walls. Team shirts. A scarf. He had favourite players too: Brendan Robson, Bryan Batson, Cyril Cunningham. He worshipped them. And United. He used to follow them on TV and the radio. But his dad didn't like him going to watch them.'

'So why is he stopping me from playing?'

'He's not, is he?' Mum said. 'Yet.'

Yunis said nothing.

'Your grandad didn't like him going because he was afraid for him. Football was different then. People like us weren't really part of it.'

'Like us?'

'Only white people went to the football. Mostly,' Mum explained.

Yunis nodded. 'So . . . he never went to watch United then?'

'He did, a few times.' Mum leaned forward again.

'I don't understand,' Yunis said.

'He's never told me exactly what happened,' Mum said. 'But he gave me a good idea of it. Do you know what I mean?'

46

'The other United fans were racist to him?' Yunis guessed.

'Not really, no. Not directly. It was more that the rest of them never let him feel like he belonged, as a fan.'

'So he stopped going?'

'Not at first,' Mum said. 'But in the end, yes. He decided to go back to watching it on TV and listening on the radio.'

'How old was he?'

'Sixteen.'

Yunis felt weird. He had never thought of his dad as a boy. He just saw him as a man telling him what to do. That's how it had been recently.

Now he actually felt sorry for his dad.

'Since then,' Mum said, 'he's always been wary of football. You can see – can't you – that he thinks your education is more important than all that?'

First-Team Player

Yunis was shattered the next morning.

After talking to Mum, he'd got to sleep about 2.30 a.m. Then he'd had to get up at ten to seven, for school.

Sitting in class, he found it impossible to listen to the teacher talking about how blood moves around the body. The words sounded like a foreign language: *vena cava, pulmonary artery, platelets.*

All he could think about was that his

dad used to be a United fan. He couldn't
believe it. He stared out of the window.
How had Dad hidden that from him? Yunis
had been a United fan since he was six.
And now he was a player for them. But
Dad had never said a word.

At the end of the class, the teacher, Mr
Baird, held Yunis back.

'Can I have a word please, Yunis?'

'Yes, sir?'

Mr Baird was a nice teacher. Not

into shouting and making threats. Yunis assumed he wanted to ask him about his school work or something.

'Is everything OK?' Mr Baird said. 'I noticed you look a bit . . . distracted today.'

'Sorry, sir. I didn't sleep last night.'

'Everything OK at home?'

Seeing as Mr Baird was asking, Yunis felt like saying something to him. Would he listen to all the stuff about his dad, the football, his school marks? Yunis almost spoke up, but then decided not to. What could Mr Baird do to help?

'Everything's fine, sir,' Yunis said.

'Well, you know where I am if you need to talk, Yunis.'

Mr Baird handed Yunis a sheet – a black-and-white picture of a body, with the heart and the veins drawn inside.

'Yes, sir.'

'And here's your homework. I'm not sure you heard while I was telling the others: you have to colour this in. Red for arteries. Blue for veins.'

'Thanks, sir,' Yunis said, then he walked into the corridor, into a stream of students pushing their way to their next class.

The next day Yunis was sitting in an out-of-the-way corridor at United, next to a fire exit, colouring in the sheet Mr Baird had given him. He'd taken a book called *The Body* out of the school library for help, seeing as he'd been too tired to listen in class.

He was sitting on the ground, feeling the hard floor through his trousers, his legs angled up so he could lean on them. It wasn't very comfortable. There was a breeze coming underneath the fire escape.

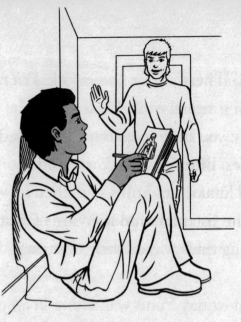

Yunis was colouring the sheet when he
heard footsteps. He immediately felt that he
shouldn't be there and that someone was
coming to tell him as much.

He'd expected to see one of the
coaches, but it was a man in faded jeans
and a sweatshirt.

'All right, son. Have you seen Steve?
Steve Cooper.'

Yunis nodded and pointed back up the
corridor. He couldn't speak. Not to Matt

Wing. *The* Matt Wing. United's leading scorer. And England international.

'Cheers, kid,' the player said. 'You should watch it. It won't do you any good sitting there in that draught.'

Yunis listened to Matt Wing's footsteps fading. Then he heard more footsteps. He braced himself for another conversation with the famous player.

But it wasn't Matt Wing: it was Craig.

Craig was carrying a school exercise book. He saw Yunis and grunted hello.

Yunis nodded at him, but didn't smile.

'What are you doing here?' Craig said.

'Nothing.'

'Looks like it,' Craig said.

'What's it got to do with you?' Yunis asked.

Craig looked at Yunis and muttered something under his breath.

'What was that?' Yunis said, putting his hand down, so he could get to his feet.

'I said . . .' Craig went on. Then he stepped back. 'Forget it. It's not worth it.'

And Yunis listened to Craig's footsteps fading away. Then he looked down at his biology drawing, scowling, completely unable to concentrate on what he was supposed to be doing.

Boxed In

*I*t was raining by the time training started. Yunis could feel the water, cold on his legs.

After they'd warmed up – three circuits of the pitch, running forwards, backwards and sidewards – Steve put them into groups of four.

There were four boxes painted in white on to the grass, measuring five metres square. Each group of four boys had a box.

'Right, lads,' Steve said. 'Here's the drill.

Three of you have to keep the ball. The other has to get it off you. Whoever loses the ball is next in the middle. You must stay in your box. Never let the ball out of the box. Ten minutes. OK?'

Some of the boys nodded.

'The trick is to use the space you've got. Use both feet and practise quick, short passes to keep control of the ball. Got it?'

Yunis was with Ryan, Sam and James. Sam offered to go in the middle first and

was immediately racing around the box, jumping in front of the ball. With his second touch, Yunis let the ball drift out of the box.

Sam grinned.

'Right, Yunis. You're in the middle,' Steve said.

Yunis could hear laughter and shouting from the other three boxes as he tried to get the ball off the others in his box. But he couldn't get near it.

He lunged at Sam, then James. But they just skipped out of his way and played the ball past him.

It was hopeless.

Ryan was laughing. 'You're slower than my gran, Yunis. And she's been dead for two years.'

Yunis saw James and Sam laughing too.

There was something about today. He felt like everything that he did was going wrong. All he could do was keep trying. Trying to close the ball down.

But at least he was here. With the team. Playing football. Yunis started to laugh too, picturing Ryan's gran coming out of a graveyard to beat him to the ball. Laughing made him even worse, so he gave up all together and watched the others.

Then he heard an adult voice. Not Steve, but two of the dads talking loudly, away to the left. Laughing too. Most of the parents were sitting in their cars, out of the rain. But two of them had bravely come to watch anyway.

Yunis looked round to see Craig's dad laughing and James's dad slapping him on the back. Two huge figures, soaked, standing in the rain.

That just about did it for Yunis. Craig's dad was here, getting drenched. *And* he was mates with James's dad. Mates with a former England player.

Yunis felt that feeling in the pit of his stomach again. All the laughter gone.

'Here you go, Yunis,' Ryan said, tapping the ball close to Yunis. Yunis went for it, determined to get it now. But Ryan dragged the ball back and flicked it sideways to James. No matter what Yunis tried, he still couldn't get the ball.

Craig's Secret

'**A**re you OK?'

Jake had caught up with Yunis in the car park. Asking that question again.

'Fine,' Yunis said.

'No you're not,' Jake said.

'I am.'

'You're not.'

'I'm the leading scorer of a Premiership academy side,' Yunis said. 'I'm an expert on the works of William Shakespeare. My

best friend is the internationally known
winger Jake Oldfield. What could possibly
be wrong?'

'Is it Poland?' Jake asked, ignoring
Yunis's sense of humour.

'What about Poland?' Yunis replied.

'Isn't your dad going to let you come to
Poland? Is that why you look so miserable?'

Yunis stopped walking. He stood there,
gazing around himself, everyone else
getting into cars, the cars moving off, the
noises of their engines fading away.

'It's everything,' he said.

'What?'

Yunis explained. The stuff about school and the Academy. How he was terrified his dad would pull him out of United. How he always felt like each game was his last and he had to make the best of it. That Poland was the least of his worries.

As Yunis was speaking he saw Craig and his dad getting into their car.

'And then there's Craig,' Yunis said.

'What about him?'

Yunis sighed and looked up at the trees that surrounded the Academy.

'He's doing my head in. He gives me funny looks, mutters at me. Half the time I think he's laughing at me. And he swans around with his dad, like he's got it made. Just because his dad comes to the football and mine doesn't. He's rubbing my nose in it.'

'He won't be,' Jake said. 'Craig's all right. Really!'

'Look at him though. I'd just like it if one day his dad didn't come to a match – or even training. Then he'd maybe understand what I feel like every week.'

'But he wouldn't see his dad otherwise,' Jake said in a quieter voice.

'What? Of course he would. They live in the same house, don't they?'

'No,' Jake said, 'they don't. His mum and dad split up. A year ago. The only time his dad's allowed to see him is when he brings him to United and takes him back.'

'Really?'

'Yeah. His mum doesn't talk to his dad. He told me. So he's only allowed Sunday and the two training evenings. He wouldn't see him otherwise.'

'Right,' Yunis said.

He didn't know what to say. Suddenly
he understood a bit more why Craig was
like he was. Especially around his dad.

Off

The Sunday game was away. To Hull City.

Yunis had been feeling bad about Craig since Jake had told him about his mum and dad splitting up. He'd tried to imagine what that would feel like. And even though his dad annoyed him, he thought it must be the worst thing that could happen.

So, when he saw Craig at Hull City, he tried to be friendly.

'All right, Craig?' he said.

But Craig just nodded, saying nothing.
And now Yunis felt even worse.

But on the pitch, as usual, Yunis was free
of all his worries. If he could really get
stuck into the game, he would forget – even
forget that this could be his last game, if his
dad decided it.

So he decided to play as if it *was* his last
game.

He worked as hard as he could.

He went into every tackle and header as firmly as possible.

And he ran and ran and ran.

It felt good.

But Hull were good too. Their defenders were huge – like grown men. It was hard to challenge for the ball.

Yunis noticed Craig getting more and more wound up on the pitch. One of the Hull defenders kept pulling his shirt when the referee wasn't looking.

'Ref?' Craig kept saying.

But the ref was giving him nothing.

A few minutes later, the defender pulled Craig to the ground, but still no free kick was awarded. Craig snapped. Getting up, he lunged at the defender with his shoulder and pushed him over.

The ref saw it.

Yunis watched the ref pull out a card.

Yellow. Yunis had been worried it would be red. Even so, he imagined Steve would take Craig off now to let him cool down. But Craig stayed on.

A couple of minutes later the same Hull defender went up for a header and clearly went for the man – Craig – and not the ball. Craig fell in a heap. But again the referee waved the play on.

Luckily United still had the ball and

James quickly slid it to Yunis, who found himself on his own up front, with only two defenders and the keeper to beat. He knocked the ball to the right of the first defender and raced past him. The second defender was trying to cover Jake, who was approaching from the left. So now Yunis was in loads of space.

Taking the ball to the edge of the penalty area, Yunis focused on the ball and hammered it as hard as he could.

The keeper didn't even move.

The ball screamed like a heat-seeking missile into the back of the net. And Yunis heard the usual cheers from the touchline.

One–nil.

James came over and clapped him on the back. Jake and the others too.

And then Steve *substituted* Yunis.

He waved to get the ref's attention.

Then shouted, 'Yunis. Come off.'

Yunis trudged to the touchline. He couldn't believe it.

'What's up?' he asked Steve.

'Brilliant goal, Yunis. You've done us proud. I want to give one of the other lads a go.'

'But . . .' Yunis checked himself. He'd never disagreed with Steve before. And he wasn't going to start now.

But he just couldn't understand it. Why was he coming off? If anyone, Craig should be coming off. He'd been booked, hadn't he? He was a liability, looking like he'd be sent off.

Yunis put on his tracksuit and did some stretches to warm down.

Then he watched the game, trying to keep himself from giving Steve questioning looks.

What Are You Looking At?

Outside the Hull City dressing room, Yunis was waiting for Jake. Jake's dad was giving him a lift home, as his own dad couldn't make it.

But it was Craig who came out next, looking hot and bothered.

Yunis was still feeling annoyed with him. Mostly because he'd tried to be nice to Craig earlier – and Craig had snubbed him. And partly because he'd been substituted when he thought Craig should have gone off.

Yunis watched Craig, but didn't speak.

'What are you looking at?' Craig said.

'Nothing,' Yunis said.

'Nothing? Is that what you think.'

Yunis remained silent.

'Shame you got subbed today,' Craig said, smiling.

Yunis stared at Craig. His anger was growing. Craig was taking the mick now. No doubt about it.

'It should have been you,' Yunis said.

'Yeah?'

'Yeah.'

Yunis knew what was going to happen next. He'd seen other boys doing this. This was how it always started. A war of words, then worse.

He'd never had a fight before, but now his body was so full of anger, his arms and legs felt like they were being pulled by ropes. Towards Craig.

'Why should it have been me, Yunis?' Craig said, stepping forward. 'Are you going to tell me? Or are you going to run home to your daddy? Or don't you have one?'

That did it. Yunis lost his temper.

Never let anyone make you lose your temper, Dad would have said. *Never hurt anyone. Words are just words.*

'At least . . .' Yunis stopped himself. He didn't want to say something that would hurt

Craig. Even though he felt like he hated him now.

'At least what?' Craig stepped forward and pushed Yunis on the chest.

Yunis stumbled backwards. And was suddenly aware that they were surrounded by other lads, mostly from the Hull City team. All eyes on him. He was embarrassed and afraid. He couldn't just stand there.

'At least I live with mine . . .' he spat out breathlessly.

He regretted it immediately.

Under-twelves manager's marks out of ten
for each player:

Tomasz	7
Connor	6
James	7
Ryan	7
Craig	6
Chi	8
Sam	6
Will	6
Jake	8
Yunis (subbed for Tony, 70 minutes)	8
Ben	7
Tony	6

School Surprise

'Yunis? Can I have a word, please?'
Mr Baird intercepted Yunis as he was leaving the classroom.

Yunis nodded. What was it now?

He wasn't really bothered that his teacher wanted to talk to him. In the last twenty-four hours he'd had his dad moaning at him about his schoolwork, Craig pushing him and Steve at United unhappy about him and Craig nearly having a fight.

It almost felt right that his teacher was

angry with him. About something.

'Are you having a difficult time at the moment?' the teacher said.

Yunis stayed at his table as all his classmates filtered out to break.

'I'm OK, sir,' Yunis said.

'It's just . . .' Mr Baird said. 'Well, your dad has been phoning the school. Checking to see how you're doing. The headmaster has been asking me questions.'

Yunis nodded.

'And I . . . well, I know you've been taken on at United. And . . .' Mr Baird paused.

Yunis looked at him. How did Mr Baird know about that? Yunis had always kept it a secret. He didn't want people at his new school knowing he was on United's books. He was too afraid he'd not make it through the first season, then everyone would know he'd failed.

'And I thought it must be hard. With your studies. Training twice a week and playing on Sunday. And your dad . . .'

Yunis stared at Mr Baird. So, how *did* he know? About training being twice a week? And that they played on Sundays?

Mr Baird smiled. As if he knew what Yunis was thinking.

'I'm a United fan, Yunis,' he said. 'A bit

too much of a United fan. I have been since I was a kid. I don't just follow the first team. I keep an eye on the youth teams too. And I know a couple of the coaching staff down at United.'

Yunis felt strange. This was the first time anyone had even treated him with

respect. Because he was a United player. Even though Mr Baird was his teacher, he felt like for once an adult wasn't treating him like a child.

'My dad doesn't like it that I go to United. He thinks it's getting in the way of my studies.'

'I see.'

'I think he's going to pull me out,' Yunis went on.

'No wonder you're upset,' Mr Baird said. 'Listen. Is there anything I can do? Talk to your dad? Help with school?'

'I don't know, sir,' Yunis said.

'What about using the library after school? Before you go to United?'

'It's too noisy,' Yunis said. 'It's more of an after-school club than a study period.'

'I see,' Mr Baird said.

Yunis looked at his teacher. He felt slightly happier. At least someone was *trying* to help him.

'Well, let me know if there's anything I can do. You're a student here *and* a future United star, so I've two reasons to help you now.'

On the Bench

Sunday.

Bolton at home.

Yunis looked up at the team sheet on the wall in the entrance to the Academy. As always. It was part of his match-day routine.

Then he stepped back in shock.

He looked again.

His name was *not* on the team sheet. In his place: Tony Harrison. Then he saw *his*

name. At the foot of the page. Among the substitutes.

It was strange watching the game from the sidelines. Hard not to start running towards the ball if Sam or Chi played it out to the wing near where he was standing. And it was more than strange to see the way Jake was linking up with Tony Harrison.

Yunis couldn't understand why he'd been dropped. He was playing better than he ever had. He was scoring most of the team's goals. He was getting 'man of the match' every week.

So why was he on the subs' bench?

United were two up by half-time. Tony had scored one. Jake the other. Jake had pointed at Yunis when he was celebrating his goal.

That made Yunis feel a bit better.

So did seeing Craig getting booked. He'd never realized what a dirty player Craig was. Forever going in too hard. Missing the ball. Taking the man.

Yunis saw the parents on the other side of the pitch.

All of them shouting support. All of them saying the right things to their sons, except Ryan's mum, who was overdoing it as usual. All of them thinking their son was the next England captain in the making.

Yunis watched them closely.

And for the first time, he wondered if he belonged here. Maybe his dad was right. Maybe he should think more about his lessons.

Who was really going to make it as a player out of this lot?

None of them probably.

Maybe one or two of them would get a run of first-team games for United. And the rest in the second division. If they were lucky.

He was wasting his time just stood on the touchline. Not even playing. He could be doing his homework now. It was in his bag. Back in the dressing rooms.

At least you'd be achieving something.

That was his dad's voice in his head again.

Just after the second half kicked off – Jake and Ryan running rings round the Bolton defence – Steve came over to Yunis.

'I wanted to tell you why you're not playing today, Yunis,' Steve said.

'Right,' Yunis said, trying to look positive.

'You're clearly having a good run. Playing very well. But I wanted to give Tony H. a chance. And I thought you could handle it. Your confidence is up. Or it should be. And I *will* bring you on for the last twenty.'

Yunis listened, saying nothing. Normally he accepted everything Steve said. But today he was furious. He thought Steve was wrong.

Drop him? While he's playing well? It was stupid.

'I was going to ask, Steve . . .' Yunis said.

'What's that, Yunis?'

'If I could go and get changed. I don't

want to play. I don't feel too well.'

Steve looked at Yunis carefully. 'Of course, son. Get changed. Get some warmer clothes on.'

Yunis sat in the dressing room, frustrated, trying to grapple with *Macbeth*:

> *That which hath made them drunk,*
> *hath made me bold:*
> *What hath quench'd them, hath given*
> *me fire.*

Reading this stuff was a bit easier now – once he'd gone over it three times. But when he had to read new pages, it felt nearly as hard as it had on day one.

He was just making some notes on a pad when he heard footsteps. At first he thought it could be Steve, coming to see if he was OK.

And then he saw Craig. His shirt off, hanging at his side.

'Is it over?' Yunis said, trying to be civil.

'I got sent off,' Craig said. 'Second bookable offence.'

Yunis said nothing. He didn't want to upset Craig any more.

Craig looked at Yunis's notebook and the copy of *Macbeth*. Yunis thought he was going to say something, but he just paused, looked sad, then turned and went into the showers.

Sunday 30 October
United 2 Bolton 0
Goals: Tony, Jake
Bookings: Craig (two yellow cards – sent off)

Under-twelves manager's marks out of ten for each player:

Tomasz	7
Connor	8
James	6
Ryan	8
Craig (sent off, 74 minutes)	4
Chi	7
Sam	8
Will	6
Jake	8
Tony	9
Ben	6

Fight!

'Right, lads.'

Steve Cooper stood with his hands on his hips.

Another Monday. Another training session.

'I want to continue working on the close passing,' he said. 'I think the work we have done recently has really paid off in the games against Hull City and Bolton. So let's do some more of the same.'

The coach put the squad into groups

of four. Different groups, as always, so they didn't get used to just playing with the same people.

'Jake, you go with James, Yunis and Craig,' Steve said, throwing Jake a ball.

Yunis frowned. He didn't want to play with Craig. It was just too tense between them.

But, strangely enough, Craig was all right.

When Yunis was doing well – with

passing and intercepting – Craig said 'Well done' and 'Nice one' to Yunis, just like he was to Jake and James.

So when Craig came over at the end of training, Yunis thought everything was going to be OK. Even after what had happened after the Hull City game.

But he was wrong.

'I saw you with your book during the Bolton game,' Craig said, gripping a set of flags he was carrying for Steve.

Yunis said nothing for a while. They were walking across the fields and over the bridge. Then towards the dressing rooms.

So, Yunis thought, *Craig has just been biding his time. Waiting until he could have a real go.*

Yunis said, 'And?'

'I'm just saying. It's funny to see you doing school work at the foot–'

Yunis stopped walking suddenly.

So suddenly that Craig knocked into him with the set of corner flags.

Yunis pushed him away.

'You think it's funny?' Yunis said. 'What's funny about it? That I got dropped? Or that I want to do well at school?'

Craig tried to speak, but Yunis went on.

'It's none of your business what I do,'

Yunis shouted. 'Just because your dad's here
with you . . .'

'No, I'm . . .'

Then Yunis pushed Craig again. And
before Yunis could do anything to stop it,
Craig was on top of him.

Yunis wasn't sure how it had happened.
Just that suddenly they were on the floor.
But neither of them was hitting. They
were just holding each other's arms, rolling
around.

Yunis could hear the chant of 'Fight . . .
fight . . . fight . . .' from boys who were in a
younger team. And all he could think was,
I'm having a fight. I'm having a fight.

And then, suddenly, he was on his feet,
pulled away. By Ryan, it turned out. And
James had Craig, holding him back.

Yunis felt like a child. A small boy being
pulled away from danger.

'What are you doing?' Ryan said, still holding Yunis back.

'He . . .' But that was all he could say. He was so angry and hyped up that he couldn't speak.

'If Steve saw that he'd kick you both out,' Ryan said. 'Out of United.'

'So what?' said Yunis. 'Let him.'

'Right,' Ryan said with a captain's authority. 'Both of you. Go in there. You've got two minutes before Steve makes it

across the fields and gets back here. Sort
it out. If you start fighting again, I'll tell
Steve. And he'll release you. Got it?'

Yunis and Craig were bundled into the
dressing room.

The door slammed behind them.

Friends?

'**I** was trying to be nice,' Craig said, after a long silence during which neither boy had even glanced at the other.

'Nice?' Yunis was still angry. But he looked up at Craig.

'Yes, nice.'

'How was that nice: taking the mick out of me reading in the dressing rooms?'

Craig had got to the root of Yunis's problem. And Yunis didn't like it. But he could tell Craig was trying to sort things out. And they had less than two minutes before Steve came back and then they'd be in trouble. Big trouble.

'I wanted to say . . .' Craig said. 'About my dad . . .'

'I'm sorry about what I said about your dad,' Yunis said. He knew he should say something back to Craig. Something kind. He thought it would help them out of this mess.

'At home,' Craig went on, 'after my dad left, my brother sort of took over. He never sees my dad. But . . .'

'That can't be easy,' Yunis said.

'It isn't. I can only see Dad so many hours a week. And that's used up by him bringing me to the football. So I never see him otherwise.'

Craig looked at his hands for a moment.

'So, back to my brother, he . . .' Craig paused again. 'The reason I said something about you reading was that, because my brother's such a . . . you know.'

Yunis nodded. 'Is he older?'

'Yeah,' Craig said. 'And he thinks he's my dad now. More like my boss even. He doesn't give me a minute's peace. So, I can never do my homework.'

Yunis frowned.

'My dad used to keep him from giving me a hard time,' Craig went on. 'When he lived with us.'

'Can't you go to your dad's?' Yunis said.

'No, he's only allowed that time with me. They went to court and he has to do what they say.'

'What about your mum?'

'She's barely there. She's got two jobs. One all day. Then she works in a pub in the evening.'

Yunis was feeling really bad about Craig now. He'd thought he was an idiot, a troublemaker. But he was wrong.

'That's hard,' Yunis said.

'And that's why I was looking at you reading. I'd been thinking I could do the same thing. Do some homework after I got sent off. I knew I wouldn't be able to do it when I got home.' Craig smiled.

'Listen,' Yunis said. 'I'm sorry about what I said. But I didn't know. It must be a nightmare at home.'

'It's all right,' Craig said. Then he looked at Yunis. 'What about *your* dad?'

Yunis shrugged. 'He's not happy with me being at United.'

'Why not? Isn't he a United fan?'

'No, he's . . .' Then Yunis smiled. 'He used to be. But he thinks it stops me doing my school work.'

'So you end up doing it in the dressing rooms?'

'Something like that,' Yunis said.

'He's probably only doing it because he's worried,' Craig said.

'I suppose.'

And then the rest of the lads came in. Closely followed by Steve Cooper.

'All right, lads?' Steve said, looking at them like he knew something was going on.

'Yeah,' Craig and Yunis said together.

Ryan and James looked at each other and shared a smile.

Dad's Idea

'How was training today, Yunis?'
Dad asked him this with no
hint of criticism. No anger or
worry in his voice. Just a question.

The family were eating dinner. In the
dining room again. Yunis's sister was out at
a friend's house.

Yunis looked at his mum. He saw her
smile as she lowered her face.

'It was good, thanks. I got to know
Craig a bit better.'

'Good,' Mum said. 'You're making friends.'

Dad was nodding. And Yunis wasn't quite sure what was going on. His dad was different. Being nice. No pressure.

'Your dad's had an idea,' Mum said.

Yunis looked up to catch Dad eyeing Mum.

Now he knew there was something going on. This was a set-up. His mum and dad had planned something and this was their softly-softly way of telling him what it was.

But, on the other hand, this was better than his dad being cross with him all the time. And the threat of being pulled out of the Academy.

'What's that?' Yunis said, trying to sound interested.

'You know I get frustrated about the time you lose between school and the Academy?'

'Yes, Dad.' Yunis stayed calm. 'I know. And I understand.'

'Well, I've been talking to my work colleagues and they're willing to let me work from home in the afternoon on training days.'

Yunis nodded.

He didn't know where this was going. He started to feel a bit worried.

'So I think . . .' Dad said.

'If Yunis is happy,' Mum added.

'Yes, of course,' Dad said. 'So we think
. . . that I could come to collect you from
school. At three. Then run you home. For
3.20 p.m. And set off for the Academy at
5.30 p.m.'

'Then you'll have two hours in the
afternoon, Yunis,' Mum said. Her voice was
insistent. That meant Yunis had to agree to
this.

'Great,' Yunis said.

It did sound OK. He'd still be at
United. He'd have time to do some
homework. And his dad would be happy.
It *was* a pain getting two buses to United
from school, hanging around at the
Academy without somewhere he could sit
and work properly.

'And I'll sort you out a sandwich. You

can eat it as you work. Yes?' Mum said.

'Yes,' Yunis said. Then he felt his mum's eyes on him. He looked up. She was looking at him like she was staring down the barrel of a gun.

And Yunis realized what she wanted.

'Thank you, Dad,' Yunis said. 'That's very kind of you.'

'It's OK, Yunis,' Dad said. 'I think this will work for all of us.'

Craig's Idea

Yunis was at school when his mobile phone buzzed in his pocket.

He looked at the screen.

'Craig?' he said to himself. 'Why is *he* texting me?'

The message *was* from Craig. Yunis had all the other lads in the team on his mobile contacts list. Steve Cooper had asked them to. So they could stay in touch on away-game days.

GOT AN IDEA. MEET B4 TRAINING?
CRAIG

Yunis texted back.

OK. SOON AS.
Y

Yunis grinned. Things were looking up. He was friends with the boy he thought was his worst enemy a week ago. His dad was

happy with him at United. And school was getting better.

It felt great.

At last, he thought. *Everything is going well.*

After his final class, Yunis jogged down the school drive to see his dad, as promised, waiting at the bottom.

'Hey, Dad.'

'Hello, Yunis. Good day at school?'

'Great, thanks.'

'Right. Let's get you home.' And with that his dad pulled out on to the main road.

'We'll get on to the ring road,' Dad said. 'Be home in twenty minutes.'

'Great,' Yunis said.

But as they turned on to the ring road, Dad's face changed.

'Oh no,' he said. 'Look at the queues.'

Two lanes of traffic were tailing back as far as they could see. Horns were beeping in the distance.

Yunis's heart sank.

After fifteen minutes of crawling along, during which Dad said nothing, he turned off, left, on to a smaller road.

'We'll try and take a short cut. Up through Old Chelsea.'

Yunis nodded vigorously. He wanted his

dad to see that he agreed with what he had decided to do. With *anything* he decided to do. But the smaller roads were gridlocked too. Yunis's dad was not the only one who'd thought a short cut through Old Chelsea would be a good idea. After over thirty minutes on the smaller roads, Dad edged the car back on to the ring road.

It was over an hour since they'd left school. And not much over an hour before they would have to leave for the Academy. And that was if the traffic was good. Dad said nothing for the next ten minutes. But Yunis could see him gripping the steering wheel, his knuckles going white.

Yunis took out *Macbeth*. He started to read, to try and make his dad less angry. But still Dad said nothing.

Once they got home, they collected Yunis's sandwiches and left immediately for

the Academy. No time for work. No time to eat. Just time for Mum and Dad to have a short conversation on the doorstep.

They drove back the way they'd come. More traffic jams. More roadworks. More hooting horns. But silence from Dad. Yunis would have preferred him to be shouting. Silence was worse. He wanted to know what his dad was thinking. But he found out soon enough, when they arrived at United.

*

'Yunis?' Dad said.

'Yes?' This was it. Yunis knew it. He cast his eyes out across the training fields, through the trees.

'I'm sorry. But this is your last time here. After today, I want you to stop coming to United.'

His dad was staring down at his knees as he said this. Yunis looked at him, tears forming in his eyes, then running down his cheeks.

Last Time

Yunis went into the building, like he normally did. Through the glass doors, past the reception desk. But the Academy seemed different to him. Like it had the day he came here for his trial.

And he realized why.

Everything was in sharp detail for him today. Because *today* was the last day he would see any of this.

There was no sign of Craig, so Yunis went straight to the dressing rooms. He thought he was the first, but James was sitting there.

They got changed together and went out to the pitch early for a kick about.

As they left, they heard Ryan taunting Tomasz again. Outside the dressing room.

'Speak English, Tomasz. You're in England now. You can't expect us to learn Polish.'

'I wish Ryan would lay off Tomasz,' James said.

Yunis nodded. He agreed.

'You're quiet today,' James said, as they walked over the bridge towards the pitches.

For ten minutes Yunis and James played long balls to each other, using the width of a pitch. James's passing was amazing; the ball landing at Yunis's feet every time. Yunis concentrated on trapping the ball, then playing it back to James, all with quick movement of his feet.

It felt good to be here, in control of a football, playing better than he ever had, playing with the son of an England international at United's Academy.

He couldn't believe it was nearly over.

They played a full game in training. Eight-a-side.

'Right, lads,' Steve Cooper said. 'I want

a quick game. One touch. No dribbling. Just pass and move. Use the skills we've been building up with the short passing.'

Craig had arrived with Steve, just as the training session was about to begin.

'I'll talk to you after,' he said to Yunis.

Yunis nodded.

The game was great. All the work they'd done on passing paid off. Yunis played up front with Will. Half the time the one-touch game led to his side losing the

ball. But the other half of the time it led to swift attacks that the defenders couldn't deal with.

The best moment was when Yunis knocked the ball to Chi, who knocked it to Will. Because Yunis had moved forward, his back to the goal, Will played it back to him. Yunis played the ball first time to James, then dropped his shoulder to spin round his defender. James played it to Will again, who slid the ball to Yunis, ten yards out.

Yunis hit the ball.

'Great goal,' Steve said. 'Stop the game.'

Steve gathered everyone in a huddle. 'That was perfect. Well done, Yunis. All that passing and movement. The best defences in your age group would struggle with defending that.'

Yunis grinned and looked across at the parents. He checked them. One by one. Was his dad there? Had he come to see him play at least once?

No, of course not.

Craig jogged over to Yunis as the team made their way back to the dressing rooms.

'I talked to Steve,' he said breathlessly.

Yunis was feeling sick. He still hadn't told anyone that this was his last time here.

'Listen,' Yunis said. 'I've got something to tell you.' He was surprised it was Craig he was going to tell. He thought it would be Jake.

'No, you listen,' Craig said. 'I had this idea. I asked Steve if we can use one of the classrooms? The ones they use for the over-sixteens.'

'I'm leaving,' Yunis said.

But Craig hadn't heard him and carried on talking. 'And Steve said yes, that we can have one of the rooms. Any time from three until six. The two nights we have training.'

Yunis looked at Craig. He felt something welling up inside him. Something he'd not felt for days, even weeks.

Hope.

Football People

'**M**r Khan?'

Yunis's dad looked up from his laptop to see a man in a tracksuit tapping on his car window.

He immediately felt the anxiety he always felt around football people. Like he was a boy again.

But he opened his door and stepped out of the car.

'We've not met,' Steve said. 'I'm Steve Cooper. Yunis's team manager.'

The two men – both so important to Yunis – shook hands.

Yunis's dad thought Steve must want to talk about Yunis leaving. He thought that perhaps he was going to try to persuade him to reconsider.

'I wanted to talk to you about the boys' idea,' Steve said.

Yunis's dad nodded, hesitantly.

A part of him wanted to smile. Yunis had come up with some idea, some scheme

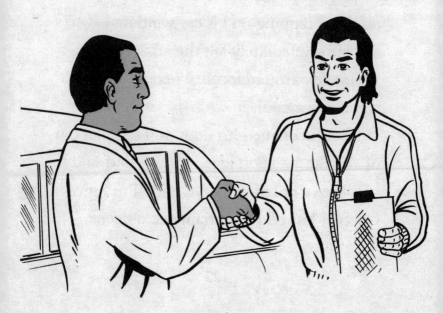

to stay at the Academy. This was one of the things he loved about his son – for always thinking of a new way of doing something.

'I'm sorry,' Yunis's dad said. 'What idea? I –' He was about to tell Steve that he was withdrawing Yunis from the Academy. But Steve broke in.

'The idea that he and Craig . . . you know Craig?'

Yunis's dad frowned. 'No, I'm sorry . . .'

'That Yunis and Craig use one of the classrooms here. For two hours before training to do their school work. I know it's a concern of parents. Maybe more of the lads will do it.'

'That *is* a good idea,' Yunis's dad said in surprise.

Suddenly he felt happy. He'd been

sitting in the car for two hours feeling awful after seeing his son so sad. And regretting being so rash after the traffic jams.

'Yes,' he said again. 'That is a very good idea.'

'Good,' Steve said. 'Also, I wanted to confirm . . .'

But Steve stopped talking. Yunis's dad wasn't looking at *him*. He was staring over his shoulder.

Steve looked round. The man Yunis's

dad had been staring at was James's dad, talking to some of the other dads.

'Do you know Cyril?' Steve said.

'Cyril?' Yunis's dad said.

'Cyril Cunningham?'

Yunis's dad nodded vigorously. 'I do. Well, I know of him. It's just I haven't seen him for twenty years.'

'I'll take you over . . .'

'No,' said Yunis's dad quickly. 'You were saying.'

'Yes,' Steve said. 'About Warsaw. Can I confirm that Yunis is *not* coming? Just for my paperwork?'

'Warsaw?'

'The trip?' Steve said. 'To Poland? To play the tournament?'

And Yunis's dad understood immediately what had happened. The team were going on a trip to Poland. And Yunis had been too scared to ask him if he could go.

As he watched Steve walk back to the Academy, Yunis's dad leaned on his car.

He had some thinking to do.

Free Kick

Yunis lined up the free kick.
Twenty yards out. Four men in
the wall. The keeper standing to the
right of the goal.

He felt good. Really good.

At last the fear that his dad was going
to pull him out of United had gone.

They'd talked about it after the training
session on Wednesday, when Dad had had
his chat with Steve. And Dad had loved
the classroom idea. Yunis had been ripping

through his homework ever since, thanks
to Craig. He felt like he really could keep
up with his school work and be at the
Academy. No problem.

It didn't matter so much that his dad
didn't come to the matches like the other
dads did. It was enough that he had his
parents' support. It would be nice to see
them at the sidelines, of course. But he
couldn't have everything, could he?

He eyed the goal.

The referee blew his whistle.

This to equalize against Liverpool. And keep their recent unbeaten record of the last few games.

He ran up to the ball and hit it low on the right side, putting some curve on it. He wanted to send it round the wall and into the other side of the goal to where the keeper was standing.

It worked like a dream. Round the wall, no problem. Then dipping into the goal.

But the keeper spotted it and raced across his line, diving, stretching for the ball.

The ball hit the ground and bounced up . . . over the keeper's hand and into the net.

Craig was the first to come over to Yunis.

'Brilliant, mate. Brilliant.'

Jake too. Then Ryan and Sam and James and Chi.

Yunis looked over to the sidelines and saw Steve looking at him, but pointing across the pitch to the opposite side. Yunis thought he meant that they'd over-celebrated the goal. But then he noticed Steve was actually gesturing that Yunis should look in that direction.

Yunis stared at the mums and dads as

he was jogging back to take up his position for the restart.

What was there to look at?

There was Ryan's mum, her arms folded. Probably annoyed Ryan hadn't been able to take the free kick himself.

There was Jake's dad. Smiling, as usual.

And there was *his* dad.

Yunis stopped running. Stopped dead still. His dad was clapping. And when he saw his son looking at him, bewildered, he raised his hand. A wave. A wave that meant the world to Yunis.

'Come on, son,' the referee said. 'Are you going to stand there all day?'

Yunis waved back, to see his dad turn and start talking to James's dad. He wondered if his dad knew he was talking to his hero from twenty years ago.

Proud

The game ended one–one. A fair result.

But Yunis wouldn't have cared if they'd won, drawn or lost. He just wanted to talk to his dad. Thank him, maybe. Something.

But he couldn't see him.

His heart dropped in his chest. Had he imagined his dad standing on the touchline?

Then he felt an arm around him.

At first, he thought it was Steve. But Steve was walking ahead of him, talking to Ben and Ryan.

Yunis looked up.

It was his dad.

'That goal you scored, Yunis.'

'Yeah?'

'That was great. Really great. I never knew you were so good . . .' Dad stopped speaking.

Yunis could have said, 'That's because

you haven't been to watch me.' But he didn't. He didn't need to make his dad feel bad. There was no point now.

His dad walked, still with his arm round him, all the way back to the dressing rooms.

'Dad?'

'Yes?'

'Do you know who you were talking to at the side of the pitch?'

'James's dad?'

'Yeah.'

'Why do you ask?'

'It's just Mum told me about how you used to go to United. And how Cyril Cunningham was one of your h– favourite players.'

'Heroes.'

'Yes, heroes.'

'I did. Steve Cooper introduced us. We talked.'

'What did he say? Was it good to talk to him?'

'It was very good, Yunis,' Dad said. 'And do you really want to know what he said to me?'

'Course I do.'

'He said that my son is one of the best strikers he's seen at under-twelves level. And that I should be very proud. That my son could have a great future.'

Yunis said nothing for a minute. Then turned to his dad.

'And are you?'

'What?'

'Are you proud?'

'Yes. I'm proud, Yunis. I'm proud you've done all this. Without any support from me. And I hope, if you'll let me support from now on, that you can keep going.'

Yunis beamed.

This was a good day. A very good day.

'And Yunis,' Dad said.

'Yes?'

'I've given Mr Cooper a cheque. I'd like you to go to Poland. If you want to.'

'You're joking?' Yunis said.

'Do I joke?' Dad said.

Yunis stopped and thought. Did his dad joke?

No.

'No,' Yunis said reluctantly. He didn't want his dad to think he was being critical. But he wanted to be honest too.

'Maybe I should start then,' his dad said.

And the two of them walked, side by side, to the dressing rooms, just like all the other boys and their parents.

Sunday 6 November
United 1 Liverpool 1
Goal: Yunis
Bookings: none

Under-twelves manager's marks out of ten
for each player:

Tomasz	7
Connor	8
James	8
Ryan	7
Craig	7
Chi	8
Sam	6
Will	6
Jake	6
Yunis	8
Ben	6

Thank Yous

The Football Academy series came about
thanks to the imagination and hard work of
Sarah Hughes, Alison Dougal and Helen
Levene at Puffin, working with David
Luxton at Luxton Harris Literary Agency.
Thanks are due to all four for giving me
this opportunity. Thanks also to Wendy Tse
for all her hard work with the fine detail,
and to everyone at Puffin for all they do,
including Reetu Kabra, Adele Minchin,
Louise Heskett, Sarah Kettle and Tom

Sanderson and the rights team. Thanks
also to Brian Williamson for the great cover
image and illustrations.

I needed a lot of help to make sure the
academy at 'United' was as close to an
English football club's academy as possible.
Burnley Football Club let me come to
training and matches at their Gawthorpe
Hall training ground to watch the under-
twelves. Vince Overson and Jeff Taylor
gave me lots of time at Burnley and I am
extremely grateful. I was also given excellent
advice by Kit Carson and Steve Cooper.

Ralph Newbrook at the Football
Foundation, also a former youth player
for Cambridge United, gave me loads of
advice and read the finished manuscript. He
– more than anyone – has helped me make
this book and series more realistic. Thank
you, Ralph!

Huge thanks to my writing group in Leeds – James Nash and Sophie Hannah.

Mostly though, thank you to my wife, Rebecca, and daughter, Iris, for putting up with the irregular hours an author keeps. I have to go away a lot – either to do events or in my head, working on the stories – and you are ever-supporting.

**STAY ON THE BALL WITH
A PREVIEW OF UNITED'S
NEXT EXCITING CHALLENGE**

THE REAL
THING

The team is off to **Poland** for a tournament.
Goalkeeper **Tomasz** can't wait to play in
his home country, but captain **Ryan** thinks
Poland are rubbish.

Can **Ryan** and **Tomasz** tackle their
differences – or will Ryan's **bullying**
foul United's chance of **success**?

Tough

After ten minutes of the game, it was still nil–nil. United had done well. Rangers could pass the ball, but they'd not got behind Ryan and his defence.

'They're not so good,' Ryan said to Ben after the ball had gone out for a throw-in.

Ben laughed. 'Easy,' he said.

James went to take the throw-in, standing close to the halfway line.

Ryan ran casually to trap the ball, but a Rangers player came out of nowhere, beating him to it. Ryan tried to take his legs, but he was too quick.

Once he had the ball, the Rangers player – a huge blond boy – took two strides and passed the ball to a team-mate. Then he was running. His team-mate looked up, saw his run and fed the ball back to him. Suddenly the blond player was in the penalty area, already past United's two central defenders, Ryan and James.

Tomasz had no chance.

The striker clipped the ball over him as he ran out to close down the angles.

As the Rangers players wheeled away to celebrate, Ryan could hear Steve shouting his name. He tried not to listen, but couldn't avoid his deep booming voice.

'Ryan . . . concentrate . . . teamwork.'

He could also hear his mum shouting. Again.

Ryan's mum was difficult – *forever* shouting at him, the referee and other players, telling them what to do. He could just imagine what she'd be saying. He shut the voices out and jogged over to Tomasz.

'You're not playing for Legia Whatevertheyrecalled now, Tomasz,' Ryan said. 'You should have closed the striker down. There was time to.' He was angry. His thoughts short and sharp.

Tomasz said nothing. He knew Ryan was at fault for the goal. He should have been marking the blond striker more closely.

Look out for

THE REAL THING

in Puffin Books